*Plea Of The Damned 3
Forgive Me Jena*

*For the quiet heroes. Particularly the ones who
put themselves on the line to save others. And
for the ones who need saving.*

# Plea Of The Damned 3 Forgive Me Jena

Avril Sabine

Cracked Acorn Productions
Australia

Plea Of The Damned 3: Forgive Me Jena

Published by

Cracked Acorn Productions

PO Box 1365

Gympie, Queensland 4570

Australia

978-1-925131-82-6 (Kindle)

978-1-925131-83-3 (EPUB)

978-1-925131-84-0 (Print)

Genre: Young Adult Urban Fantasy/Paranormal



Cover design by Caitlyn Petersen

*Plea Of The Damned*

Have you ever done something and immediately wished you could undo it? Jack knows that feeling very well. He's damned, bound to haunt his old school and help students until he atones for his sins. It's the last thing he wants to do. But since the alternative is an eternity in hell, he's not about to say no.

*Book 3: Forgive Me Jena*

As the anniversary of her dad's death approaches, Jena is visited by a ghost who says he's there to help. All she wants from him is contact with the ghost of her dad, refusing to believe he can't help and unable to accept her life is in danger. Her life is too ordinary for her to ever be in danger. Things like that happen to others. People, like her father, who put themselves at risk to keep everyone else safe.

*

This story was written by an Australian author using Australian spelling.

## *Chapter One*

*Jack*

Jack looked out across the school hall, watching the students dance, the music far different than what was played at the dances he'd once attended here. The music might have been different and the clothes certainly were, but the expressions on the faces hadn't changed. Couples gazing into each other's eyes, girls laughing, boys nudging each other and giving significant looks to their friends as a way of encouraging them to make a move and other students trying to blend into the shadows, looking uncomfortable with being at the dance.

It was the year eleven dance and the hall was filled with sixteen-year-olds. Had he ever looked like that guy in the corner, staring longingly at one of the girls huddled with a group that kept sending rather obvious looks to a group of boys not far from them? When Rose had dumped him, had he stared at her like that? With a hopeless, lovesick look. He stepped away from the wall he stood near, sighing heavily. It was best to forget the past and focus on the future. If a ghost could be considered to have a future. He strode through the crowd, about to step outside, stopping when he saw the angel in the doorway. It had been over two months since he'd last seen him. Long months where he'd tried not to complain in case the blasted bird was deliberately making him wait to see how patient he was. It wouldn't have surprised him if that were the case.

He managed not to speak any of the bitter words that wanted to pour out. "Who is it this time?"

The angel gestured to a girl in the arms of a boy who was a couple of inches taller than her. "Jena."

He really tried not to ask any questions, already knowing the angel wasn't about to answer them. "What's her problem?"

"I'm beginning to think you're a lost cause." The angel slowly shook his head, a disappointed tone in his voice.

Jack barely managed not to point out that the blasted bird had always felt that way. "Leaving me in the dark isn't doing them any favours."

"Nor would telling you their problems."

The angel vanished and Jack was left glaring at nothing. Muttering under his breath he faced the dancing students, trying to find Jena. It didn't take him long. She was dancing with the same boy.

While Jack watched, she laughed at something her companion said and he grinned down at her. She had medium brown hair, hanging past her shoulders and pinned back on one side with a couple of decorative clips. Jack tried to think of a way to describe her face and could only come up with it being both angular and soft. Her brown eyes remained on the boy who held her and her dress clung to her slim figure.

Jack checked over the boy, deciding he didn't look like he'd be much use in a fight. Although he supposed looks could be deceiving and the boy's long sleeved shirt might hide a wiry strength, but he doubted it. Neither of them looked to be the sporty type. The boy's hair was several shades lighter than Jena's and his blue eyes glinted with humour, his smile remaining in place.

Jack found himself slowly shaking his head like the angel had before. They looked too young. Had he ever looked so naive? He doubted it. At least not after he'd lost his mother. Pain filled him at the thought of Elizabeth as he'd last seen her, tears streaking her face as she knelt beside his dying body, already long dead herself. He tried to pull himself away from old memories, but like the sound of gunshot he'd never been able to forget, they clung to him, playing over and over again in his mind.

One stupid mistake. Well, it had been more than one he supposed. An entire series of them had led up to the moment he'd accidentally shot Rose. He doubted Rose would ever forgive him no matter how much he atoned for his sins, which was why he was stuck at his old school helping students with their problems. He wanted Rose to forgive him. He loved her. Even after all these years. But he knew he didn't deserve her forgiveness, no matter how much he might wish it.

Forcing the memories away, he focused on Jena. What could she need help with? The chick looked like she hadn't a care in the world. He guessed he'd soon find out. Hopefully not before it was too late. He didn't need any more failures to dwell on. There were more than enough of them already. Probably as many as the sins he had to atone for.

*Chapter Two*



*Jena*

Jena stepped outside, holding onto Korbin's hand, the cool night air making her wish she'd worn something warmer. But then she'd have been too warm, during the dance, with the heated building and the students all crowded together in the hall. "Wait here for me. I won't be long." She started to move away from Korbin.

He took hold of her hand, drawing her back. "Where are you going? My brother will be waiting out the front to pick us up. You know how he hates waiting."

His brother was a pain, but at least he had a licence and could be bribed to give them lifts. "I forgot some stuff in my locker that I need for an assignment that's due next term."

"The one due on the first day back at school?"

She grinned. "Yeah. That's the one."

"If you get caught they'll give you detention. That wouldn't be something to look forward to after the June-July holidays. No wandering around the school during the dance will include getting something from your locker."

She shrugged. "I'll blame forgetting it on the upcoming anniversary of my dad's death." It had taken her a lot of years to be able to speak about it like that. As if it didn't matter and was unimportant. Eleven years. A pity the way she felt didn't match her tone.

"I'll come with you."

"Not likely. Then I would get in trouble. They'd think we'd snuck off to make out."

Korbin chuckled softly. "As tempting as that sounds, my brother would kill me for making him wait so long." He took his phone out of his pocket, checking the time. "I'll tell him you won't be long so he doesn't drive off without us."

"Okay." She started to pull away again.

Korbin drew her back to him, kissing her before he let go. "Five minutes."

"Plenty of time." Turning away, she broke into a run, stumbling slightly in her high heels. She slowed, not wanting the night to end with her sprawled across the ground because she'd tried to run in the wrong footwear.

It didn't take her long to reach her homeroom and take the papers out of her locker that was situated out the front of the classroom in the middle of the row. Luckily all the lights were on throughout the school grounds, making it easy to find what she needed. Closing and locking it, she turned away to stop at the sight of a boy standing not far from her. She didn't recognise him. He had dark eyes and black hair, wore a white t-shirt with a black leather jacket and blue denim jeans. There was an old fashioned look about him, like he wished he could have lived in the late 50s or early 60s of the previous century. She took a step back and her shoulder collided with the lockers.

"You don't have to be afraid. I don't plan to hurt you."

As reassuring as he sounded, she didn't believe him. "Then walk away." He was between her and the direction she needed to go in.

"Let's see if I can manage this without freaking you out."

She stepped away from the locker, taking another step back to put more distance between her and the boy. "I have to go. People are waiting for me. My boyfriend and his brother." Should she kick off her high heels and run? Her mum had told her they were impractical to wear in winter. It looked like that wasn't the only reason why they were impractical.

"Maybe one day I'll figure out how to say this without sounding completely off the wall. I'm Jack Richards and I died in 1963 on my eighteenth birthday. I was killed here, at this school."

Just her luck. "You seriously need some help." She remembered her mum talking to her stepfather about a shooting when she'd first started high school here. "Why would you want to pretend to be some shooter from the 60s when there's more than enough school shootings in the world without some lunatic glorifying them." She tried to remember all the details of the story. The guy had shot his girlfriend and her new boyfriend, but she couldn't remember how he'd died. She hadn't really paid much attention.

He looked surprised. "You know about me?"

She half shrugged, eyeing the distance between them. "My mum's a bit of a history nut. She's got to know the history of everywhere we go." Her five minutes had to be up. The last thing she wanted was Korbin to come looking for her and try and be a hero. Images of her dad in his uniform came to mind. At best, heroes got hurt. Usually they died.

"Well, that's good. You won't need me to tell you what happened."

"I have to go." She glanced over her shoulder, wondering which would be the best escape route.

"I've been sent to help you. And judging by my previous assignments, there's a good chance your life will be in danger."

She nearly laughed. "You're the only danger I can see around here."

"I already told you, I'm not here to hurt you."

Before she could say anything, she heard Korbin call out her name. She was torn. Did she call out a warning? Try and run past Jack? Before she could decide, Korbin came running towards her, straight through Jack.

"I hate when they do that," Jack said.

She couldn't stop staring at Jack.

Korbin stopped in front of her, resting a hand on her shoulder. "Are you okay? You look like you've seen a ghost or something."

Jack chuckled. "I wonder how many times people have said that without actually knowing how true their words were."

She couldn't drag her gaze from Jack. She felt five-years-old again, racing to answer the door, her mum on her heels telling her to leave it alone. An army officer had stood there, his hat in his hands and a solemn expression on his face. His words had made no sense and her mum had screamed at him that he was wrong. Her husband always returned. Jena had raced to her room and grabbed her dad's favourite jacket, taking it to the front door to show the officer.

She'd held it up. Every time he'd left, he'd drop his jacket around her shoulders and said, 'Keep it warm while I'm gone. I'll be back to collect it.' She'd met the officer's hazel eyes, continuing to hold up the jacket. "He said he'd be back for his jacket. I'm keeping it warm for him." She'd wrapped it around her shoulders, holding his gaze. The officer had cleared his throat and looked from one to the other, asking if there was someone he could call for them.

Korbin shaking her shoulders dragged her back to the present and she realised Jack was standing close, echoing Korbin's question of if she was okay. She shook her head then nodded, realising they'd probably take it the wrong way. How could Korbin not see Jack? She was obviously losing her mind. Why hadn't it happened years earlier? When she'd first lost her dad.

"Jena?"

She managed to drag her gaze away from Jack to stare into Korbin's troubled blue eyes. "I thought I saw something. Or someone." She glanced towards the parts of the school grounds that were in shadows. "Let's get out of here." She deliberately didn't look towards Jack.

"You okay? I shouldn't have let you come alone."

"Don't forget to come and see me when you need help," Jack called after her.

She kept walking, slipping her hand into Korbin's. "What could you have done if someone had attacked?" He wasn't much stronger than her.

Korbin grinned, not in the least offended. "You don't think I'd take someone on alone. It's two of us. Two against one sounds like better odds to me."

She returned his smile like he expected, but it felt forced. The same sort of smile she'd used in the early years when they'd begun to assume she should be getting over it. How did you get over losing someone you loved? How did you get over losing your hero?

# Chapter Three

Jena

When they reached the car, Jena slid into the back, ignoring the complaints that came from the front and Korbin trying to placate his brother. Looking out the window she saw Jack in a pool of light at the front entrance of the school. Several students walked through him, heading for their own ride home. She shivered. Jack couldn't be possible. If ghosts were real, why hadn't her dad returned to see her? When she'd finally accepted he'd died, even though there'd been no body to bring home, she'd begged and pleaded for him to come see her one final time. For him to reach out to her from beyond the grave so she could say a final goodbye. It was the year her mum had remarried. The year she'd turned nine.

The moment the car pulled up in front of her

house, she said a hurried thanks and clambered out of the car. Korbin joined her on the footpath, walking with her towards the front door. She kept her gaze on the light by the door, not sure what to say. How were ghosts possible?

"You sure you're okay?" Korbin faced her when they reached the front door.

"Yeah. I guess I got a fright. Schools normally seem like a safe place." She thought of the girl who'd died in 1963, shot by her ex-boyfriend. "I suppose they aren't always."

Korbin slid his arms around her waist and drew her closer, keeping some distance between them so the paper she held wasn't crushed. "I wish I didn't have to go with my family these school holidays." He grinned. "Or that your mum would have let you come too."

This time her smile came easier. "Yeah, not likely." She leaned forward and kissed him, drawing away when the car horn sounded. "I better let you go before your brother wakes up the entire neighbourhood."

He started to draw away then came close again for one last kiss before he strode to the car.

She stared after him, watching as he got in the car. She raised her hand, when he waved, as his brother drove off. She didn't go inside until she could no longer see the glow of the taillights in the distance. The lounge room light was on and her mum was lying on the lounge chair, a book open on her chest and her eyes closed.

Jena tried to close the door softly, not wanting to wake Patrice. She managed that task, it was the sound of the lock clicking into place that had Patrice blinking sleepily. "Sorry, Mum. I didn't mean to wake you."

Patrice sat up, her book sliding to the floor. She tried to grab it before it closed. It landed on the floor with a thud. Leaving it where it landed Patrice ran fingers through her short hair, the same shade of brown as Jena's, before rubbing at green eyes. "I didn't plan to fall asleep. I wanted to ask how the dance was."

Jena forced a smile to her lips, trying not to think about Jack. It didn't help. He intruded anyway. "Good."

Patrice shifted over and patted the seat beside her. "Come and tell me. Who was that girl that was caught smuggling alcohol into the year ten dance last year and threw up on one of the teachers? Was she there?"

A smile came easier this time and she kicked off

her high heels, leaving them by the front door. She left the paper, she was holding, on the coffee table before sitting beside her mum. "No, she was the one who got expelled earlier this year. Before the year had barely started."

"What did happen then?"

An image of Jack came to mind and her smile faded once more. "Do you have photos of the boy who killed his girlfriend at the school?"

Patrice looked startled. "Yes. He was in all the newspapers. Such a sad story. What makes you ask?"

She shrugged, unable to give the real reason. She didn't want that worried look to return to her mum's eyes. Her mum had worn it for years, like she'd worn the jacket day and night for far too many years. "Just something that happened which made me think of it."

"What happened?" Patrice's voice was sharp. "Korbin didn't do anything, did he?"

"Mum." She drew the word out. "Not likely."

"It's not completely unthinkable. Sometimes people don't turn out to be who we think they are."

"Korbin is exactly who I think he is. We were friends for years first." Initially it had felt weird dating her best friend, but it hadn't taken long for it to become as natural as their friendship. "It's nothing to do with me. Or Korbin." At least she hoped it was nothing to do with her. She couldn't get Jack's words out of her mind. 'Don't forget to come and see me when you need help.'

"Okay. If you're sure." Patrice didn't continue speaking until Jena nodded. "So what did happen at the dance tonight?"

"Nothing. Seriously. Nothing happened. I spent most of the night dancing with Korbin. Or doing what he calls a dance." She grinned, remembering how the majority of the night had been spent swaying to music while wrapped in his arms. She rose to her feet. "It wasn't boring, but nothing interesting happened. Night, Mum."

Patrice picked up her book before standing. "Sweet dreams."

She stared at her mum for a moment, remembering the years when that had been more of an order than a habit. Years when she hadn't managed a single night without being woken numerous times from nightmares. "Can you email me all the research you did on the shooting?"

"What about the rest of the file I put together on the history of your school?"

She nearly said yes at the hopeful expression on her mum's face, but that would mean she'd have to wade through what was probably several gigabytes of data, to find the bit of information she wanted, if she accepted. "Only the information on the shooting."

Patrice's expression fell. "All right. I'll do that in the morning. Be careful not to wake your brothers going to your room. Their bedroom door is open."

With a nod, she entered the hallway that led to the bedrooms. She reached the bathroom first, stopping to use it before walking past her brothers' room. When one of them made a noise, she turned back to check. They looked nothing like her. With their sandy brown hair and freckles they looked like Colin, their father. Her stepfather.  Hayden, the oldest at seven, was sprawled across his bed with one arm and leg hanging over the edge. In the other single bed five-year-old Albert, who'd been named for her dad, was curled up in a ball, the teddy he always denied taking to bed wrapped in his arms. They were far less annoying when they were asleep.

Not wanting her mum to catch her staring at them and have her asking more questions, Jena hurried to her bedroom and softly closed the door as she flicked on the light switch. Changing into her pyjamas, she tried to tell herself it was all because of the upcoming anniversary of her dad's death. The rest of the year she was okay. In the weeks leading up to the day that had changed her life, eleven years ago, she couldn't help the unsettled feeling that formed.

Jack was a part of that. Ghosts didn't exist and when she saw the photo of him tomorrow she'd prove that to herself. Turning off the light, she climbed into bed, the sheet cool against her feet. She was tempted to get a pair of socks, but tiredness settled over her and she snuggled further into the blankets. Luckily tomorrow was not only Saturday, but the start of the school holidays and there was no reason for her to get up early. She could sleep as long as she liked. Her last thought before drifting off to sleep was of Jack's words. 'I've been sent to help you. And judging by previous assignments, there's a good chance your life will be in danger.' The only danger she had to worry about was that of losing her mind.

# Chapter Four

*Jena*

Jena was dragged from sleep hours later by a nightmare, her room dark. Staring at the glowing numbers of her alarm clock, she turned on the bedside lamp. So much for sleeping in. It was half past four and after the nightmare she'd had there was no way she'd fall back to sleep. Once she'd used the bathroom she tried to focus on reading a book. All she could see, imposed over the words of the story, was images from her nightmare. She'd been plagued by them for so many years. All of them had featured explosions, dead bodies and her dad calling out for help.

Giving up on reading she turned on her laptop, that sat on the desk in the corner of her room, pacing the floor as she waited for it to load up. Finding no friends online and unable to focus on any of her favourite games, she rose from the seat and crossed the room to stare down at the framed photograph on her bedside table.

She reached out, hesitating a moment before she picked it up. A solemn man stared back at her, black hair neatly combed, brown eyes looking into the camera and wearing an army uniform. In his arms was a smiling four-year-old girl, wrapped in his favourite jacket. While he faced the camera, she faced him. It was taken the year before he'd died. He'd been twenty-nine-years-old in the photo. That was only thirteen years older than she currently was. It wasn't fair. She tossed the photo onto her bed and crossed the room to the built-in wardrobe, dragging out the jacket she'd worn in the photo.

Slipping her arms into the sleeves, the fabric well-worn, she wrapped it around herself. It wasn't fair. She'd spent more than half her life without a dad. Shutting the wardrobe she sat on the floor, leaning against it. It just wasn't fair. She closed her eyes on the tears that wanted to escape and emptied her mind, focusing on her breathing. She kept focusing, unable to think about her dad this close to the anniversary of his death. She had no idea how long she sat there, trying to regain control, but was pretty sure it hadn't taken her long. Not like it had in the early years.

Before she had a chance to check the time, a message came through on her phone. It was from Korbin. *Last message before we leave civilisation and phone coverage behind. I miss you already and can't wait till these holidays are over. I'll see you on the Friday before school starts.*

She smiled. This was exactly what she'd needed. She didn't know how he did it, but Korbin was often there for her just when she needed him. She quickly typed in a message in the hope he'd get it before he lost coverage. *Are you sure it isn't the internet and gaming you'll really miss?*

*Is this one of those questions where there's no right answer?*

She tried to hold back her laughter, not wanting to wake anyone this early in the morning. *I miss you too.* She waited, but there was no reply. Hopefully he'd managed to get the message before he'd lost coverage. She leaned back against her wardrobe, her eyes closing as she thought of Korbin. When his parents had started planning this holiday, she'd wanted to go too. Her mum had said no. Absolutely no. And all her pleading hadn't helped.

A ping from her computer letting her know she had a new email had her rising to her feet, startled to find it was after six. She'd completely lost track of time while trying not to think about her dad. Something she hadn't done in ages. Losing track of time when she was doing something fun didn't count.

She made her way to the desk and sat down in front of her laptop, checking her emails. There was one from her mum. Relief rushed through her. Now she'd be able to see that last night had only been her imagination. She clicked on the file, tapping her fingers on the desk as she waited for it to download, opening it up the moment it did. Ignoring most of the information, she scrolled past it until she found a photo. It was slightly grainy, but more than clear enough to show her the truth she didn't want to recognise.

Her mouth went dry and her hands began to tremble. She clasped them together in an effort to keep them steady. How was this possible? Would he be able to get in touch with her dad? Could Jack ask him to come and talk to her? The initial fear faded and excitement raced through her. There were so many things she wanted to tell her dad. Questions she wanted to ask him.

She continued to stare at the screen. Ghosts were real. Goosebumps rose on her arms beneath the jacket and she rubbed at them. Standing, the chair nearly fell over and she grabbed at it. What was she doing sitting around here? She needed to see Jack.

It took her longer than she liked to get ready. Her mum had been hard to convince, especially when she saw her wearing the jacket. Then she'd been expected to have breakfast before she left on her supposed bike ride in a sudden desire to get fit these holidays. She hadn't been able to think of any other reason why she'd want to be riding around the streets of Brisbane on a Saturday morning when she usually tried to sleep in. But it wasn't like she could explain what she was really going to do. Korbin hadn't seen Jack and she had a feeling her mum wouldn't be able to either.

When she was nearly ready to leave, having been slowed down by trying to find her bike helmet since her mum wouldn't let her leave without it, her brothers woke. They'd begged to go bike riding with her. It was only Patrice's reminder that they were going out for pizza that night and had they thought about what toppings they wanted that the boys were distracted long enough for Jena to escape.

As she came closer to her school, her pedalling slowed. What was she going to say to him? And what if she couldn't find him? Worse, what if he wanted to have nothing to do with her after the way she'd treated him last night? She was still worrying over that thought when she reached the school. Stopping at the main entrance, she dismounted and left her bike propped against the fence, the helmet hanging from the handle bar. Jack could be anywhere.

It took her a few minutes to work up the nerve to enter the school grounds. Not because she was afraid to meet a ghost, no because she was afraid he wouldn't help her. She had no idea what she could do to convince him if he refused.

Before she'd gone very far into the school grounds she saw Jack striding towards her, wearing the same clothes as he had the previous night. She stopped, unable to take another step, wrapping her arms around herself. He had to say yes. He had to.

Reaching her, Jack glanced around. "What happened?"

"You're real, aren't you?" She reached out towards him, gingerly pressing her fingers against his chest. He felt so solid.

"As real as a ghost can be." His tone was dry, his lips momentarily twisting into a mocking smile. "What made you figure it out? Think it'd help me to convince other people when I need to?"

She shook her head. "I doubt it. I saw a picture of you in an old newspaper. If it had come from anyone else other than my mum, I wouldn't have believed it. I would have thought they'd photoshopped it or something."

"Pity." He gestured towards the way he'd come. "Let's get out of the open before someone starts wondering why you're talking to yourself."

She glanced around, not seeing anyone.

"We're alone. For now. But this place sometimes gets busy on the weekend. You'd think you would get enough of the place during the week without wanting to spend your weekends around here."

She fell in beside him. "Where are we going?"

"Groundsman's shed."

"Won't it be locked?"

"Yeah, usually. Hopefully that won't be a problem today."

She remained silent, wanting to be somewhere private before she tried to convince him to help her. Like he'd already pointed out, she didn't need anyone she knew coming along and finding her talking to herself. Not with her dad's anniversary so close. Reaching the groundsman's shed, she tried the handle. "It's locked."

"Not for long." Jack walked through the door. He came back out. "Blasted thing." He walked back through the door again and this time the sound of the lock clicking could be heard.

# Chapter Five



Jena tested the door handle of the groundsman's shed. It was unlocked. She stepped into the dark interior and took out her phone to use the flashlight app. Closing the door she shone the light around the dark interior in time to see Jack walk through an old wardrobe on the far side of the room. Somehow it seemed more eerie in the barely lit room then in the sunlight, the only light being what crept in under the door. She remained frozen on the spot until the app timed out and the room darkened further. Fumbling with her phone she turned the light on again, this time keeping her finger on the screen to prevent it from turning off. She tried to remind herself that she'd known Jack was a ghost. That she thought it was great. But seeing him walk through a wardrobe in a shadowy room had caused goosebumps to rise on her arms and a chill to travel down her spine. Ghosts should be impossible.

Taking a deep breath she shone the light over tools, broken furniture, stacked boxes and cluttered shelves, making her way through the crowded shed. Reaching the corner she saw there was a gap between the wall and the wardrobe. More than large enough for her to slip sideways between the two. Entering the small area behind the wardrobe she found Jack sitting on the floor, leaning up against the wall with his leg drawn up to rest his arm on.

Jack gestured towards a brown cushion that lay on the floor beside him. "It's not very warm in here, but at least you won't have to sit on the cold floor."

Her gaze was drawn to the photocopied picture on the wall just above her eye height. A smiling girl stared at her. "Who is this?"

"Rose."

He sounded like the name should mean something to her. It took her a moment to realise why. He thought she knew the entire story. "The girl you killed?"

"The one who killed me." He smiled, fondness in his eyes and a mocking tone in his voice.

"You don't hate her for it?" She really needed to

find out the full story. But after. Once he'd contacted her dad for her. She sat on the cushion beside him.

"No. Never. She was defending herself."

"From you." Even though her words were a statement, she watched as he nodded. "Should I be worried?" She was tempted to move away from him, but she needed his help.

"What about?"

She reached out and momentarily rested her hand on his arm, her other hand keeping the light app turned on. He felt solid. Very real and very solid. And probably far stronger than her. "You. I don't want to die."

"Never. I already told you. I was sent to help. I have to atone for all my sins and I do that by helping the people an angel tells me to help."

"An angel." She couldn't keep the disbelief from her voice.

Jack chuckled softly. "You believe in ghosts. How much harder is it to believe in angels?"

"I don't know." Not that it mattered. She had more important things to focus on. "I want to talk to my dad."

Jack frowned. "Why can't you?"

"He's dead. I want you to tell him I need to talk to him. That's what I need help with."

His frown cleared. "It doesn't work like that. The only person I can talk to is the one I have to help and you don't get to choose what you want help with."

"You said you can talk to angels."

"One angel. And I wouldn't count him as a person."

She came up off the cushion to kneel in front of him. "Please, Jack. I need to talk to him." She stretched out an arm. "This is his jacket. Will it help to have something of his to call him with?"

"I'm sorry." His words were soft, his gaze holding hers.

"I don't want sorry. I want to talk to my dad. He promised me he'd come back. That he'd return for his jacket if I kept it warm for him. You have to call him." She wiped the back of her empty hand across her cheeks, surprised they were damp. "Please, Jack. You have to help me."

He took her hand, holding it tightly between his. "I will help, but this isn't what you need help with."

She dragged her hand from his grip. "How can you say that?"

A wry smile briefly appeared. "Because your life isn't in danger."

No, but her heart was. She could feel it shattering again. The hope that had risen in it that morning trickled away like the sand in a broken hourglass. She sat back on her legs, the cold of the floor seeping through her jeans as she closed her eyes, letting her phone fall to the floor as she wrapped her arms around herself. "I miss him so much." The words were a whisper.

"I know."

She opened her eyes to find the room dark. "How can you know?"

"Because I live with the constant thought that I killed one of the few people who ever loved me. Who I loved."

"So did I."

"How?"

She tried not to think of that day, so many years ago, when she'd yelled at her dad because she hadn't wanted him to leave. "I told him if he went away I didn't want him to come back."

"What happened?"

She turned on her flashlight app again and stared into his dark eyes. "How will it help telling you what happened?"

"I don't know."

Neither did she. Staring into his eyes, she could almost see the pain he'd talked about. A pain she was familiar with. "I was five-years-old." Some days the memory was vivid enough it felt like she was reliving the moment, unable to stop herself from saying those words she wished she'd never spoken…

## *Chapter Six*



*Jena*

Jena glared at her dad, her arms crossed over her chest as she stood in front of him. "Stay."

"Don't be like that, pumpkin." He sat in the lounge chair, his favourite jacket on the seat beside him.

"You said you wouldn't leave again until next year. It's not next year." She continued to glare at him.

"Sometimes things happen that we have no control over."

"You can tell them no. Tell them you promised."

"Now, Jena-"

She hit out at him. "You promised."

He captured her hands, holding them gently. "I never promised, pumpkin. I only said I shouldn't need to go away until next year. But there are people in countries overseas who need us. Little girls like you who might die if I don't go."

"But I miss you when you're gone."

"I know." He picked up his jacket, reaching out to wrap it around her. "Keep it warm for me while I'm gone. I'll be back to collect it if you keep it warm for me."

She snuggled into the folds of the fabric, the scent of her dad enveloping her. "You'll be gone the same amount of time as always?"

"I'm sorry, pumpkin. It'll be longer this time."

"No." She took a step away from his outstretched hand.

"I can't-"

"No. If you go I don't want you to come back."

"You don't mean that."

She glared at him, biting her lip to stop tears from falling. He had to say he'd changed his mind. He had to.

He came forward and wrapped his arms around her. "Love you, pumpkin."

She didn't reply, too angry to say the words.

With a sigh he let go, rising to his feet to tower over her. "I'll call you when I can."

She watched him step out the door, her mum having already said goodbye, not wanting to be the one to watch him walk away. It was usually Jena who stood at the front door, waving. This time she glared at his retreating figure, willing him to say he wouldn't go. But he didn't and the sound of the door closing seemed overly loud. Panic raced through her. Letting the jacket fall to the floor she ran to the door and flung it open. The taxi was halfway down the street. She was too late. She wanted to run after him. She took several steps forward, staring down the empty street.

"What are you doing outside?"

Jena turned to see her mum. "I forgot to tell Dad something." Putting her hands behind her back she crossed her fingers, hoping her mum wouldn't ask her what she needed to say.

Patrice smiled. "That's okay. You can tell him when he rings." She glanced up the street before she returned her attention to Jena. "Come inside."

* * *

Jena remained silent a moment, fiddling with her phone. She forced herself to meet Jack's eyes. "He never rang. Instead we got a knock on the door to say he'd been lost along with six other soldiers. There'd been an explosion."

"I'm sorry. I wish I could help you, but I can't."

"What about asking your angel?"

"He's not mine and he doesn't come when I call. He'd probably prefer to send me to hell rather than give me a chance for atonement."

She'd told him things she'd never told another person and still he was refusing to help her. "But-" She broke off, not sure what to say. "I thought-" Surely he hadn't been telling the truth. "You really can't contact him?"

"I'm sorry."

She rose shakily to her feet, stumbling after having been in the same position for so long.

"Jena-" He stood up, reaching for her.

She brushed his hand away. "I have to go." She took a step backwards.

"Come and see me when you know what you need help with."

Another couple of steps had her back against the wall. "No one can help me. Not unless you can bring the dead back to life." She slipped between the wall and the wardrobe, but not soon enough to miss his whispered words.

"It's something I've spent decades wishing I could do."

As soon as Jena was outside, she ran to the front gate where she'd left her bike. She reached for the helmet, her vision a blur from falling tears, her fingers fumbling on the strap as she tried to buckle it up. She couldn't go home. Glancing over her shoulder she saw Jack standing near one of the buildings. And she obviously couldn't stay here. Not knowing where to go, she grabbed hold of the handlebars and walked away, not confident that she could manage to stay on the bike.

She wandered aimlessly for several hours, heading for home once she'd managed to stop crying and cleaned her face at the tap in someone's front yard. The entire time she'd kept expecting a car to drive up and park in the empty carport and someone to get out and demand what she was doing in their yard.

It didn't happen and she arrived home well after lunch, not sure if she could face eating. In the end she made a sandwich, not wanting to have her mum asking questions she didn't know how to answer.

# Chapter Seven



Patrice entered the kitchen. "You shouldn't overdo things your first day of exercising or you mightn't continue."

Jena swallowed her mouthful. "I didn't. I ran into a kid from school and lost track of time talking." Technically he was a kid from her school, just not from this century.

"Anyone I know?"

She shook her head. "Where are the boys? It's scarily quiet."

Patrice laughed. "It's okay. They aren't plotting mischief. Colin took them to the park. He said it might be best to wear off their energy if we expect them to sit long enough to eat their dinner like half civilised beings this evening."

A reluctant smile formed. "Good plan." The smile faded. "I might work on my assignment."

"If you're looking for the paper you left on the coffee table I put it on your desk this morning."

"Thanks." Eating the last few bites of her sandwich, she headed to her room.

When she sat down in front of her laptop she ended up reading over the file her mum had sent her instead of doing her assignment. She'd worry about it tomorrow. Or the next day at the latest. She wasn't going to leave it until the last day as she had every other assignment this year. She'd promised her mum she'd be more organised and not end up staying awake the entire night before in an effort to have her assignments in on time.

Once she'd finished reading the file, she stared at the image of Jack. It was nearly impossible to believe the smiling, good-looking boy in front of her had shot his girlfriend. Harder to believe Rose had managed to stab him. Who took on a gun wielding person with their own knife? One they'd used trickery to get. She scrolled down the page to look at Rose, then further down to stare at the image of Elizabeth, Jack's mother who had died nearly a year and a half before him.

Jena ran her fingers over the image on the screen.

She knew how he felt, but unlike him, she'd had her mum to help her through the pain of losing her dad. From what she'd read, there hadn't been anyone for Jack. According to one of the articles, those interviewed had said his father hadn't been the sort to know how to deal with a grieving child. Even his own.

The sound of running feet down the hallway drew Jena back to the present. She closed down the file and rose from the chair, stretching after being seated for so long. There was a banging on her door and she crossed the room to open it.

"Mum said to get ready," Albert said.

Jena grinned at her unusually neat and tidy brother. "Strange how it's you who's ready and not holding us up for a change."

Worry filled his expression. "Aww, Jena. You wouldn't. It's pizza."

She couldn't resist laughing, reaching out to mess up his hair. "Of course not. After all, it's pizza."

He glared at her. "You're mean." With one last glare, he ran towards the other end of the hallway and their parents' room. "Mum!" He drew the word out so it sounded like it contained two syllables.

Still smiling, Jena grabbed a change of clothes and headed to the bathroom. It didn't take her long to shower and dress in jeans and a long sleeved shirt, pulling her dad's jacket back on. By the time she joined her family in the lounge room, her brothers were arguing and Colin was refereeing.

Jena stared at Colin. He was always so calm. Had been a rock when they'd lost Albert, who'd been his best friend. She'd never seen him lost for words, or unable to think of the right thing to say. Like now. The boys shuffled their feet and stared at the floor, muttering sorry to each other. She grinned, remembering times when she'd felt the same way.

There was a knock on the door and Jena crossed the room to open it, staring into solemn brown eyes that were strangely familiar. The face was worn, the black hair threaded with grey and the clothes hung on his gaunt frame.

"Jena."

The voice was so familiar. She took a step back, shaking her head. This wasn't possible. Had Jack somehow convinced the angel to grant her wish?

"Albert?" Patrice's voice was uncertain, coming from behind Jena.

She couldn't look to see where her mum was, could only stare at the man in front of her.

"What?" Jena's brother Albert asked.

"I don't think Mum was talking to you," Hayden said.

"Was too. I heard her," Albert argued.

"Al? Is that you?" Colin came to stand beside Jena.

Jena could only shake her head, hearing her brothers start to argue again. Behind her Patrice kept repeating the words 'this isn't possible' while Colin remained silent. Unusually silent. Her focus narrowed down to the man in the doorway, everything else fading. "Who are you?" Her voice was almost a whisper as she wrapped her arms around herself, the jacket doing nothing to prevent the chill that ran through her. It couldn't be possible. Jack had kept telling her he couldn't help.

"I couldn't wait. They said they'd come and talk to you on Monday. Prepare you. I couldn't wait another minute. Not after how long I was in hospital. I never should have told them not to tell you until I was well. But I hadn't realised it'd take so long. I didn't want any of you to see me in the shape I was in." He started to reach out towards her then pulled his hand back to clasp it with the other one. "I barely recognise you." Silence spun out for a moment. "You were so little when I left. But you have the same eyes. I'd recognise your eyes anywhere."

It was strange to hear him say that when it was his

eyes that had been what she'd first recognised. "Dad?" She wanted to throw herself into his arms, but was scared he'd vanish.

"Albert." Patrice stepped between Jena and Colin, crowding the space at the front door. "They said… they told me… this is impossible."

Impossible. The word rang in Jena's mind. Yes. It was impossible, but it seemed like it was the week for impossibilities. Her throat tightened and she fought against the tears that wanted to fall. She didn't want anything to obscure her vision of her dad. She struggled to take the jacket off. "I kept it warm while you were gone." Finally managing to remove the jacket, she took a step forward and held it out to him.

Arms encircled her and the jacket was pressed between them. "Pumpkin. You can't imagine how much I missed you."

The familiar endearment caused tears to form and she closed her eyes as the tears trickled down her cheeks. The moment had a surreal quality to it. As if at any moment her alarm clock would ring and she'd drag herself from bed to face another day in which her dad hadn't survived. But she'd already done that today. Had spent part of it begging a ghost to bring her dad back so she could talk to him one last time. Her arms tightened around her dad. She needed to talk to Jack. Needed to know if this was real. That her dad wasn't going to disappear on her.

"I can't believe you're here," Patrice said. "How is this possible? Albert? How is this possible?"

Before anyone could speak, Jena's youngest brother spoke. "Does that mean I can get my own name now he needs his back?"

She didn't know whether to laugh or cry and from the sounds her mum was making, Jena was pretty sure she didn't know either.

"Why don't we all go sit in the kitchen?" Colin sounded dazed and uncertain.

"What about pizza?" Hayden demanded.

Releasing Jena, her dad put his jacket back around her shoulders. "You're freezing." He stepped forward, keeping an arm around her. "You were all going somewhere?" His gaze swept over everyone.

"Do you like pizza?" Albert asked.

Jena's dad stared down at his namesake. "I love it."

The boy held out his hand. "I'm Albert. They gave me your name. But you can have it back if you want."

"Most people call me Al." He solemnly shook the boy's hand.

"Really? That's much better than Albert. Cause Albert sounds like an old man's name."

"Albert!" Colin sounded half shocked, half amused. "You're being rude."

Jena smiled, remaining pressed against her dad's side, relieved Albert was his usually talkative self so she didn't have to think of anything to say. She was still reeling from finding her dad on the doorstep.

"How is being truthful rude?" Albert looked puzzled. "You tell me I've always gotta tell the truth."

## *Chapter Eight*



Jena grinned at her brother, knowing from past experience that they'd be wasting their time trying to explain it to him.

Patrice reached out and rested a hand on her son's shoulder, her gaze drawn to Al. "Come inside, Al. We need to talk."

Al's gaze momentarily rested on Colin before he faced Patrice. "I know." His voice was soft. "They already told me."

"I'm sorry. I thought-" Patrice looked away.

"I know." Al's arm tightened around Jena. "It doesn't matter. I'm glad to be home, no matter what else has changed."

"Can I get you something to drink?" Colin asked.

Taking another step forward, bringing Jena with him, Al shut the door, shaking his head. "I'm good."

"What about pizza?" Hayden asked.

"We could order in," Patrice said hesitantly.

Jena didn't care about dinner. As long as her dad didn't leave her sight she didn't care what else happened.

"I'll order pizza. The kids need to eat." Colin drew his phone from his pocket.

"We'll sit in the kitchen. There's more room for everyone in there." Patrice took several steps towards the doorway, glancing frequently at Al.

Jena remained at her dad's side, walking with him to the kitchen. When they all sat down, she took the chair next to him, not wanting to let him go. "Where were you? What happened?"

Al met her gaze. "You know I would have returned if I could, don't you? The thought of you waiting here for me was one of the things that got me through each day."

Jena glanced towards her mum. Had she been one of the other things that had got him through each day? "I know." Like he'd said, it didn't matter. He was here now.

Conversation was broken and awkward, becoming less so when the pizza arrived. When the boys went to bed, Colin going to tuck them in and make sure they actually went to sleep, Patrice suggested returning to the lounge room. Once Colin joined them, the long awkward silences were filled with talk of people they all knew and what they were doing these days. Jena continued to sit by her dad even though the conversation bored her and she stopped listening.

As it got later, her lack of sleep had her blinking heavily and struggling to keep her eyes open. She didn't want to miss one second of her dad's return. Didn't want to sleep. Somehow, she found herself opening her eyes to see she was in her bed with the blankets pulled up, sunlight coming through her bedroom window.

Panic raced through her and she stumbled out of bed, terrified the night had been a dream. She didn't know if she'd survive losing him a second time. Flinging her bedroom door open, she raced along the hallway, through the lounge room and into the kitchen. Only her mum was there, seated at the table. She didn't know what to say.

Patrice looked up from the book she was reading. "What's wrong?"

Jena shook her head, not knowing how to ask if she'd been dreaming.

"Are you sure nothing's wrong?"

"Who put me to bed?"

"Al carried you."

Her legs felt weak. It hadn't been a dream. She leaned against the doorway. "I want to see Dad."

"He wants you to spend the holidays with him. I said no."

"What?" Surely she hadn't heard correctly.

"You can spend the afternoon with him and we'll take it from there."

Jena slowly shook her head, trying to comprehend what her mum was saying. "He's my dad."

"He's been missing for eleven years, Jena. He won't be the same man we once knew."

"I'm staying with him."

"No."

"You can't stop me."

Patrice slipped a bookmark between the pages of the book and left it on the table when she stood up. "I know how much you've missed him and how much a miracle this is, but I don't want you to go rushing into danger."

"Dad would never hurt me." She couldn't believe her mum was being like this.

"I don't know what the past decade has been like for him, he didn't say, but I imagine it's changed him. Who knows what he endured while he was held captive." Patrice reached for her.

Jena stepped into the kitchen and to the side. "When will he be here?" She didn't care what her mum said. She was staying with her dad during the holidays. And no one was going to stop her.

Checking her phone before returning it to her pocket, Patrice said, "In five hours."

"I'm going for a ride."

"What about breakfast?"

Not wanting to spend time arguing, she grabbed a breakfast bar from the pantry and headed to her room to get ready for the morning. It wasn't until she was on her bike and riding towards school that she thought to wonder where her brothers had been. The house had been far too quiet for them to have been at home. Deciding it wasn't important, she tried to think of the questions she needed to ask Jack. Demanding if he'd had something to do with her dad's return probably wasn't very polite.

Instead of heading for the front gate, she rode around to the side closest to the groundsman's shed. Leaving her bike leaning against the fence, the helmet on the handlebars, she clambered over it. Jack strode towards her before she managed to reach the shed. She stopped and waited for him.

"Did something happen?"

She grinned. "You could say that."

"Are you sure it was something good."

"My dad came home." She watched as Jack's expression went from surprise to disbelief. "It is something good." Her eyes narrowed. "It is."

"The angel wouldn't have said you needed help for no reason."

"Well it's got nothing to do with my dad."

"Is there another problem?"

She shook her head. "I wanted to know if you had something to do with him coming home."

"I've already told you I can't bring back the dead. Although I guess he wasn't dead after all. What happened?"

She shrugged. Her dad had been pretty vague about that. But she knew from experience that sometimes it wasn't possible to talk about the things that went wrong. Look how many years it had taken her to tell someone about her last moments with him. "It doesn't matter. All that matters is he's home and Mum isn't going to stop me from spending time with him."

"Why is she trying to stop you?"

She wasn't about to answer that question. Not since Jack was already looking for problems. "It doesn't matter. I'm staying with him during the holidays. It's that simple."

"Nothing is ever simple," Jack said bitterly.

She ignored his comment. "I wanted to thank you for listening to me yesterday. But everything is good now. Dad is home."

"If you can see me, then it's not good."

She started to argue, then stopped. It didn't matter. She knew. That was all that mattered. "It was…" She faltered. Saying it was nice to have met him didn't seem right. "Thanks for listening to me. I hope you can atone for your sins." She managed a smile for him before she turned and walked towards the fence.

"This isn't goodbye. I know you'll be back."

# Chapter Nine



Jena didn't bother replying, but kept walking to the fence and clambered over it. Jack didn't know her dad. It was good he was home. More than good.

Jena arrived home, with plenty of time to spare, before her dad was due to pick her up. She tried to start her assignment, but was too distracted. She'd work on it tomorrow. It wasn't every day your dad came back from the dead.

By the time Al arrived, Colin had returned from dropping the boys at his parents' place and both him and Patrice had argued with Jena about staying with her dad. She'd refused to budge and finally Colin had said they'd take it one day at a time.

Al entered the lounge room to be greeted by an awkward silence. Even Jena wasn't sure how to act around him. She half expected it all to have been a dream.

Al gestured towards the small suitcase by the front door, his gaze remaining on Jena. "You're staying for the school holidays?"

Seeing the hope in his eyes, she started to agree.

"Tonight only. We'll discuss it again tomorrow," Patrice said.

"Mum-"

"Tonight is a good start." Al picked up the suitcase. "Did you want me to ring in the morning or did you want me to bring Jena back and discuss it."

This time Jena managed to speak before Patrice could. "We'll ring." She moved towards the front door. "Bye." She swung the door open.

"Come back here and say goodbye properly."

Jena crossed the distance between them, dropping a kiss on her mum's cheek. "Bye, Mum." She looked towards Colin. "Bye." She wanted to leave before Patrice could come up with a reason to stop her.

Patrice drew Jena in for a hug before she could take more than a step. "Call if you need me. No matter the hour."

"I'll be fine." She returned the hug before retreating to the door. "I'll call you in the morning." She took a step backwards and through the doorway. "Not too early though. I might sleep in since it's the school holidays." She half turned to walk with Al to his car.

"Did you take your assignment with you?" Patrice stood in the doorway.

"I'll pick it up next week." The moment she spoke the words she worried Patrice would expect her to get it tomorrow since it was Monday. "Later in the week." She kept moving, nodding her head at the last minute instructions Patrice called out. Reaching the car, she got in the front passenger seat while Al put her suitcase on the back seat. Looking out the window she was surprised to see her mum remained at the door. Patrice hated to watch people leave.

Al opened the driver's door. "You have everything you need?"

She met his gaze as he sat beside her. "Yeah. Everything." A grin made her cheeks ache. Absolutely everything. Even her dad.

"We'll drop your gear off and I'll show you the bedroom I have for you. It's nothing fancy. We could get some stuff for it tomorrow. After we drop off your gear, I want to visit a few of my favourite places with you this afternoon. Places we went to when you were little." He started the car.

"Okay. That sounds good." Anything would have sounded good. She glanced out the window and saw that Patrice and Colin remained in the doorway, Patrice waving. She raised her hand, looking away before they were out of sight, trying to ignore the feeling of guilt. She struggled to think of something to say. What did you tell someone who had been missing for eleven years?

Al glanced towards her. "I'm renting a place not far from your school. I was hoping that eventually you could spend some of the school term with me."

"That'd be great." They had so much lost time to catch up on.

"It's not far. When they were helping me find somewhere to live, after I got out of hospital, I told them it had to be near your school. I wouldn't accept anywhere else."

"I wouldn't have minded if it was a long bus ride."

Al glanced towards her again, smiling. "You mightn't have, but I would. All that wasted time spent on a bus when we could have been doing something together." Another glance towards her. "Remember how often you talked me into taking you to the park? You would have lived on the playground equipment if we'd let you."

Jena chuckled. "You make me sound like a homeless person in the making."

Al echoed her chuckle, pulling up in front of a

lowset timber-clad house. "We're here. What do you think?"

It looked like a typical house to her. "Looks good."

"I'll show you inside." Al collected her suitcase from the back seat and led the way to the front door.

Jena followed him inside, looking around the sparsely furnished lounge room. A single door led from the room and she stepped into a kitchen. Like the lounge room, vinyl covered the floor. It took her a few minutes to figure out what the place was missing. Personal touches. It looked like no one lived here. She'd soon help him solve that problem with her tendency to leave things lying around.

"This way." Al stepped through a doorway to his right that led into a hallway. There were three doors along the hallway, a bathroom between two bedrooms, and a door at the end leading to another bedroom. Al stopped in front of the second bedroom. "This is the second biggest. I thought you might like it." He set the suitcase down to the left of the doorway.

Jena entered the room. The single bed was against the far wall, a window with flowery curtains above it. There was a built-in wardrobe at the foot of the bed and the walls were painted an off white. The room seemed colourless. Even the pale pink bedspread did nothing to improve the lack of colour. Smiling, she faced her dad. "This room will be great." Once she fixed it up. "I can't wait to get some things for it." She had no idea how much he planned to spend. "Did you have any ideas for the room?"

"I was thinking you'd need a desk. For your homework. If we can't find one tomorrow you could use the kitchen table for now, couldn't you?"

"Sure. That'd work. Shelves would be good too. And some posters."

"Yes, a nice little timber bookcase along that wall." He pointed to the wall her suitcase sat against. "What do you think of your bedspread? I know how much you love the colour pink."

Her smile nearly faltered. "I don't like it as much as I used to." She regretted the words the moment she saw his expression. "But it goes well with the delicate flower print of the curtains."

"I thought you'd like those curtains when I saw them. We could find a nice matching rug that you could put by your bed. The floor can be a bit cold on your feet in the morning."

Maybe she should have told him she didn't like the bedspread or the curtains. But she hadn't wanted to see that sad and disappointed expression again. "I guess we can see what they have." Hopefully nothing pale pink or covered in little flowers so she could use that as an excuse for different curtains and a new bedspread.

"Did you want to unpack now or when we come back? I was thinking we could eat out tonight. A celebratory meal. After we've visited one of the places we used to go to when you were little."

"I'm ready. Where are we eating?"

Al led the way to the car. "A great little restaurant I know. I bet you'll love it."

She got in the car, continuing to smile. She doubted the day could get any better than this. "I'm sure I will."

They remained silent as Al drove through the streets. Eventually he pulled up in front of a shopping centre, leaning towards Jena to peer out her window. "It's gone."

She knew exactly where he'd been planning to take her. "They tore the park down three years ago. It was going to cost too much to improve it and make it a safe place for children. There were a lot of protesters, but it didn't help." The expression on his face made her wish she could have said something else. Anything else. "The lookout is still there." They'd often gone to the lookout after the park, watching as the sun set over the city. "We could go there."

Al's expression brightened. "That's a great idea." He checked over his shoulder before he pulled out onto the street.

Once again they remained silent as they drove to the lookout, arriving before the sun had set. There were very few parking spaces left as the place was fairly crowded. Jena walked beside Al, knowing the exact location he planned to stand in. The perfect viewing spot according to him. Memories flooded her mind and her throat tightened. She'd missed so many years. So many opportunities to stand here beside him as the sun set across Brisbane, splashing it with colour as the lights came on and kept the darkness at bay.

# Chapter Ten

*Jena*

Jena slipped her hand into Al's like she'd done as a little child. His hand seemed cold. She was sure his hands had been much warmer years ago. Unless it was that her hands had been a lot colder.

"I used to think about this. Watching the day end with you and Patrice."

She'd stood between them, holding hands. Back when she'd thought the worst thing possible was the times when he'd be away for months. Only a handful of phone calls and emails to let her know he missed them too. Sorrow washed over her and she tried to recapture the initial joy. It was impossible. The moment wasn't the same. And it wasn't different because both her parents weren't here beside her. No, it was something else that she couldn't quite figure out.

The sun set and the darkness of the city was perforated by millions of lights. It didn't help. No matter how much light, the darkness crept in and touched your life anyway. She unsuccessfully tried to push morbid thoughts away. Why was she letting them intrude on her time with her dad? She should be celebrating. "It's getting cold." She looked towards Al. "We should probably have dinner. I'm used to having it early because of the boys."

Al lightly squeezed her hand before letting go. "It was nice to visit here again. That was a good suggestion."

She walked with him to the car, nodding in answer. It hadn't been a good suggestion. But she couldn't figure out why. A celebratory meal would help recapture the mood. She waited for Al to unlock the car before getting in, turning up the heater once the car was started. Maybe that was it. Early winter was a stupid time for standing on top of lookouts. That was a summer activity. Feeling warmer and relieved she'd figured out what was wrong, she stared out the window. The streets were familiar, but she had no idea where he was taking her.

Al pulled up in front of a dark shop, pressed

between two dilapidated buildings. "I don't understand. This place was thriving when I was last here."

She had no idea what to tell him. She'd never been to this restaurant and from the looks of things it had been years since the place had been open.

He hit the top of the steering wheel. "I wanted to take you somewhere special."

"We could go to the pizza place Mum and Colin were going to take me and my brothers to last night. They make more than pizza." When he continued to look disappointed, she tried again. "It's a family restaurant."

"It's your favourite place?"

She wouldn't go that far, but how could she say no when he had such a hopeful expression? "They make some of the best food I've ever tasted."

"Okay. How do I get there?"

She directed him through the streets. When they pulled up, she was relieved to see the place wasn't overly crowded. They headed for the front door, Al holding the door open for her to step inside the warm interior of the restaurant. Toby, a waiter who knew her well, came forward with a smile.

"Your parents aren't with you tonight?"

Her heart sank. "This is my dad." Seeing the shock

on Toby's face give way to curiosity, she spoke quickly. "We came here to celebrate his return."

"Of course." Toby nodded. "This way please." He led the way to a table for two, handing them each a menu. "Would you like a few minutes before you order?"

"Yes." She nearly blurted the word out, not wanting him to stay and ask uncomfortable questions. Maybe she should stop making suggestions. Neither of them had been very good.

Al stared at the menu. "What do you recommend?"

"Uhm." She stared blindly at her own menu. Why had she suggested this place? What if the owners were here? They tended to come and chat to Patrice and Colin if they were. Would they do the same to her? What would she say to them? Maybe she should try and get the meal over and done with as quickly as possible. Al didn't like to talk about the years he was missing. The owners were sometimes a little too friendly and wouldn't hesitate to ask such questions. "The pasta is really good." And probably one of the quickest meals to serve.

Al closed the menu. "That sounds good. What about you?"

"Pasta."

Toby came forward once they'd both placed their

menus on the table. It only took him a couple of minutes to take down their order. Jena watched Toby leave, trying to think of something to say to Al. When Toby returned shortly with the drinks, she was still trying to think of something. She took a sip of her soft drink. What had they talked about when she was little? She didn't have a clue, but she didn't recall there being any of these long, awkward silences.

"How's school?"

"Good." Silence fell again. "Uhm. I've got an assignment to do during the holidays." She found herself rambling about her assignment and how Korbin was stuck in a mobile phone dead zone on a holiday with his parents and that she wouldn't see him until the last weekend of the school holidays.

"You have a boyfriend?"

She had no idea what to say. Not with the shocked tone of his voice. Seeing Toby walking towards them with their meal she nearly cheered. She smiled weakly, nodding in the direction of the arriving food. "You're going to love the pasta. It's the best I've tasted anywhere."

Al waited until Toby had placed the plates on the table and left after being told they didn't need anything else. "How long have you been dating him?"

"Uhm. We've been friends forever."

"So you're not dating him."

"Well, I am now, but…" She had no idea what to say with the look on her dad's face. She wasn't quite sure what the look meant. Anger? Disappointment? Horror? A mixture of all three? "I'm sixteen. Mum said I could date when I was fifteen."

"I'll talk to her about that tomorrow."

She nearly said, 'not likely'. There was no way she'd dump Korbin. That wasn't going to happen. Lowering her gaze, she focused on her meal. "It's good, isn't it?" She gestured towards his plate with the fork she held.

"Yes."

Silence fell again and this time she didn't bother trying to break it. What could she do if he convinced Patrice that she couldn't date? Things weren't meant to be going like this. She had her dad back. Everything was meant to be perfect. As she finished her food, she came to the conclusion that they needed time. That was it. Time to get used to things. She placed her cutlery on her plate. "Thanks for this. A celebratory dinner was a good idea."

Al looked relieved. "Did you want dessert?"

She shook her head. There was no way she wanted to stay here any longer than necessary. "I'm actually a little tired. I was up early this morning." Worried it had all been a dream.

"I couldn't sleep last night either. I was disappointed when Patrice said I had to wait until so late in the afternoon to visit you again."

"If I'd had your number I would have called you to let you know to come earlier."

He took out his phone and waited for her to take out hers before he rattled it off, reading from the screen.

After she keyed in his number and told him hers, she returned the phone to her pocket. "We should go." When he nodded, she rose to her feet and followed him to the reception desk where he paid for the meal. Stepping outside she pulled her jacket tight around her. 'Keep it warm for me while I'm gone. I'll be back to collect it if you keep it warm for me.' The words played over in her mind. She'd kept it warm and now he walked beside her. Alive. It felt like a dream. How long would it take before it no longer felt like one? Before she stopped thinking he'd disappear again. She had no idea. Hopefully soon. The long uncomfortable silences were annoying.

Once again Al held the car door open for her, closing it when she was seated. He walked around to the driver's door. "Are you warm enough? It's getting rather cold now."

"I've got your jacket." She returned his smile. Things would get better. It would take time. She was a different person to the one he'd known all those years ago. Looking out the window, she remained silent, relieved when they reached Al's home. She walked silently beside him, her arms wrapped around herself against the chill of the night air.

## Chapter Eleven



*Jena*

Al unlocked the front door, flicking on the light switch as he stepped inside. "Are you sure you're warm enough?"

"Of course." Jena slipped off her shoes, leaving them by the front door. The chill of the floor against her feet had her changing her mind. "Well, I was." She looked down at her feet. "I think I need slippers."

Al chuckled. "Go have a warm shower and off to bed then. That'll warm you up." He hesitated. "Unless you wanted a drink or something. A warm Milo?"

She shook her head. "I'm okay. Shower and bed sounds good." She headed towards the kitchen doorway, glancing back at him standing by the door. He looked lost. She smiled reassuringly and guessed it must have worked because he returned her smile. Bed sounded like a good plan. They could start over again in the morning. Find something to do or somewhere to visit that still existed.

It didn't take her long to shower and climb into bed. Falling asleep was another matter. She was still awake when she heard her dad go to bed. Still awake when she heard him shout. She sat up, staring at where she knew the closed door was in the darkened room. Was he okay? Reaching for her phone she used the light app, shining it on the door. Everything was silent. Should she check? She didn't have a clue.

There was another noise. A cry of pain. She was out of bed and across the room in seconds, opening the door to peer into the hallway. All the lights were off, only the light from her phone cut through the darkness. What was going on?

"No. Don't." The words left silence in their wake.

The floor chilled her feet and she wished she'd packed her slippers. They were panda bear slippers and made her smile every time she wore them. She doubted they'd have helped her smile tonight.

"Please." The cry was filled with pain and anguish. The sort of plea you made when you knew it wouldn't be answered.

It made Jena hurry along the hallway, opening Al's bedroom door to peer into his room. She kept the light pointed at the floor, half shielding it with her hand. Al whimpered and she came forward, reaching out a hand to wake him. She'd barely made contact with his shoulder when she found herself pressed against the nearby wall, a knife at her throat and her phone on the floor, light shining towards the ceiling.

"Where are they? Tell me where they are."

She didn't recognise the harsh voice he used. It sounded like it belonged to a stranger. "Dad." Her heart thudded loudly and fear raced through her.

"Tell me." His grip on her shoulder tightened.

"Please, Dad. It's me. Jena." Her voice broke on her name.

"You can't trick me like that. Now tell me where they are."

"I want to go home." She felt the tears escape, sliding across her cheeks. "I want my mum." The light went out, plunging the room into darkness. She hadn't thought the situation could get any worse. But it did. In the darkness all she could focus on was the knife at her throat, the grip on her shoulder, the wall at her back and the harsh sound of their breathing. "Dad. Please, Dad."

His grip loosened. "Jena?"

The confusion she could hear in his voice didn't do anything to reduce the amount of fear she felt. "Dad?"

The knife clattered to the floor and his arms wrapped around her. "Never wake me. Do you hear? Never." His words were fierce, his grip tight.

"You were having a nightmare."

"Never. Understand?"

She didn't understand at all. "Yes."

He let her go, stepping away from her.

Jena blinked when he turned the bedside lamp on. "I only wanted to wake you from your nightmare." Her gaze dropped to the knife on the floor. Swallowing became difficult. The long, sharp blade glinted in the light.

"Here." Al held out her phone.

She automatically took it from him, not having noticed him move. "Why do you sleep with a knife?"

"Are you okay?" He picked up the knife and slid it under his pillow.

Her gaze remained on the pillow, the image of the knife fixed in her mind. "I wanted to wake you from your nightmare."

He placed a hand on her shoulder.

She flinched.

"I would never hurt you. You know that, don't you, pumpkin?"

She dragged her gaze from the pillow, forcing herself to meet his gaze. She stared into the familiar eyes of her dad. "I'm sorry." She threw herself into his arms, not knowing what she was apologising for. What had happened to him. Waking him. His reaction when she'd woken him. She didn't have a clue.

He patted her back. "It's okay, pumpkin. You go back to bed and forget all about this. It won't happen again."

She drew back from him. "Are you-"

"It won't happen again because you won't wake me. Will you?"

She shook her head.

"Go back to bed. We're going shopping tomorrow. We'll get some things for your room."

She could only nod, clutching her phone tightly.

"Go on then."

With another nod, she retreated to her room, turning on the light app before she closed the door. Patrice's words came to mind. 'I don't know what the past decade has been like for him, he didn't say, but I imagine it's changed him. Who knows what he endured while he was held captive.'

She rested her forehead against the bedroom door. Her mum couldn't be right. She wanted her dad back. Not someone changed beyond recognition. She didn't expect him to be exactly the same. Even she wasn't. But she couldn't stand it if he was so different there wasn't the slightest bit left of the man she'd once known.

When her legs began to give out on her, she locked the door, staggered to her bed and collapsed on it. She didn't know what to do. Clutching her phone, she looked at the screen as the light faded. She brought up her list of contacts, flicking through them. She couldn't ring her mum. What if Patrice never let her see Al again? She stopped on Korbin's name. Why did he have to be away? This was the worst time possible for his parents to have decided to take them on a holiday to a mobile phone dead zone.

She squeezed her eyes shut, trying not to picture the knife. It didn't help. The length of the blade, the way it had caught the light and the sharp edge were all engraved in her mind. Opening her eyes, she stared into the darkness. She had no idea what to do. Jack's words came to mind.

'Don't forget to come and see me when you need help.' They were followed by more of his words. 'I've been sent to help you. And judging by previous assignments, there's a good chance your life will be in danger.' She hadn't thought it was possible. Apart from losing her dad when she was five-years-old, she'd led the most ordinary of lives. Not boring, just ordinary.

# Chapter Twelve

*Jena*

Jena remained huddled on her bed, trying to sleep. She drifted in and out of sleep all night, waking with a gasp every time she drifted off, feeling the knife pressed against her throat again. The greyness of early morning had her giving up on sleep. Once again.

She dressed quietly, put her phone in a pocket of her jeans and slipped out of her room, heading for the kitchen. The chill of the floor had her glad she'd grabbed her jacket. Wrapping her arms around herself, she stared at the sleeves. They reminded her of how her dad had held her after he'd dropped the knife. She let her arms fall to her sides.

A noise had her glancing down the hallway, towards the door of her dad's room. It was closed. She had to get out of here. Needed to talk to someone.

And her best friend wasn't in town. She thought of Jack. School wasn't that far away. She could easily walk there. But what would Al say if he woke to find her gone? Another sound had fear racing through her. He was having another nightmare. She couldn't listen.

Returning to her room, she took a pen and paper from her unpacked suitcase and scribbled a note, leaving it on the kitchen table. She stared at it a moment. Was she doing the right thing? Hearing a shout from Al's room she almost ran to the front door. She hesitated. She didn't have a key. What if she needed to get back in before he woke? She was torn between leaving and staying. Taking a deep breath, she slipped her feet into her sneakers and unlocked the door. She couldn't listen to his nightmare any longer. Stepping outside, she locked the door behind herself. She would talk to Jack. He'd said he'd help.

During the walk to school she alternated between wanting to go home and wanting to stay with her dad. He hadn't really hurt her. Only given her a bit of a fright. Okay, a major fright. She hadn't figured out what to do by the time she was clambering over the fence and walking towards the groundsman's shed. Jack stood in front of the door, waiting for her.

"Did something happen?"

She started to explain, then blurted out, "Did it hurt? When Rose stabbed you. Did it hurt?"

"What happened?" He reached out to grip her shoulder.

His hand on her shoulder had her heart racing and she stepped back before she could stop herself. "I–" Her mind seemed to go blank. Well, apart from the image of the knife she could see. She had no idea how she could stop herself from seeing that same image over and over again.

"I didn't feel a thing. Not even when my body collided with the floor."

It took her a few seconds to realise he was answering her question about the knife. The information didn't make her feel any better. Her legs felt like they wanted to give way on her again and she swayed on her feet.

Jack came forward and put an arm around her waist, guiding her to the door. "Come inside and talk." He stopped in front of the door, gesturing towards it. "You'll have to open the door since I can't."

Not having any other idea of what she could do, Jena opened the door and stepped inside the dark interior. "Why me?" She looked towards Jack, who remained at her side.

He shrugged. "I don't know. He gives me the names and I try and help." He smiled wryly. "Sometimes I'm not sure why they bothered to give me a chance."

"They?"

"I saw my mum before I died. I doubt her and the angel would be the only two." He glanced towards the door, more daylight shining on his face. "Think you can shut it before someone walks past and notices it's open."

She took out her phone and turned on the light app before closing the door. She followed Jack across the room, avoiding the many items he walked through. When she was seated on the brown cushion, in the space behind the wardrobe, she haltingly told him what had happened. Several times she had to turn the light app back on when it timed out. He remained silent when she finished. She started to ask him what he suggested, but changed her mind. Did she really want to know? "You need a lantern in here. Or a light or something."

"How do you think I'm going to get one? I can't even open and close a door."

She shrugged. Before she could tell him they had one in their garage, he spoke.

"You need to tell someone, Jena."

"No."

"He could kill you."

She shook her head. "He loves me. He'd never do anything to hurt me." She'd never see him again. Her mum wouldn't let her. Look how she'd already tried to stop her from staying with Al.

Jack rose to his feet, towering over her. "Love? You think that will keep you safe?" He gestured towards Rose's picture on the wall. "I loved her. That didn't keep her safe."

She stood up, feeling uncomfortable with how he towered over her. "You couldn't have. How could you kill someone you love?"

"Do you think I meant to?" He jabbed a finger in the direction of the picture, causing it to ripple slightly. "I would have done anything for her. I couldn't imagine life without her."

She frowned trying to understand what he was saying. "So you took her with you? Or tried to?"

Jack laughed, a sound devoid of all humour. "No way. It was a lame accident. Probably the most lame one in all of history. I wanted her to come with me. But I lost my cool and everything went wrong."

"This is different." Jack had been messed up from losing his mum. She tried to ignore the thought of what Al would have endured during the past eleven years. "There has to be something else I can do. I don't want to lose him."

"Telling someone doesn't mean you'll lose him."

"You really don't know my mum."

"Jena, do you want to die?"

A shiver went through her at his words. She started to say he didn't understand, but closed her mouth. She could see it in his brown eyes that he did understand. "I'm sorry." She glanced towards the picture of Rose before meeting his gaze again.

He held her gaze a moment longer before he stared at the picture. "So am I. Every single day. Even after all these decades." He remained silent for a few seconds before he looked at her again. "Do you want your dad to live with the same regrets? Or yourself? Tell someone."

She started to argue against telling someone when his second comment sank in. "Me? That doesn't make sense. First you ask if I want to die then you ask me if I want to live with regrets."

He looked at the picture again. "She was nowhere near as strong as me. Only had a knife and I had a gun. My knife." Meeting Jena's gaze, Jack took a step closer. "I am dead because of her. She stabbed me before I shot her. Deliberately stabbed me. Me shooting her was an accident. Do you want to be in that same situation?"

Fear curled through her and she shook her head, taking an involuntary step back. She could almost feel the knife in her hand. There was no way she could use it against her dad. No way at all.

"Tell someone, Jena."

She looked away. Away from Jack and away from the picture. Her gaze was fixed firmly on the back of the wardrobe. "I can't. I don't know what I'm going to do, but I can't tell anyone." Her throat tightened and she forced herself to look at Jack. "I can't lose him again."

"I know exactly how you feel. I couldn't face losing someone else again. Instead of letting go, I lost everything. Even my life."

Goosebumps rose on her arms at his words. She wrapped her arms around herself, her gaze drawn to the sleeves of the jacket, her phone half hidden by the folds of the material. Her breath caught in her throat at the memory of Al's arms wrapped around her after he'd dropped the knife. "There's got to be another way."

"You know there isn't."

## *Chapter Thirteen*



*Jena*

The phone rang and Jena made a sound that wasn't loud enough to be called a scream. Hand shaking, she stared at the name on the screen. Dad. She sank to the floor, unable to move the short distance to sit on the cushion. The cold seeped into her body as she answered. "Hello, Dad." The greeting sounded too ordinary.

"What are you doing sneaking out of the house?"

For a few seconds his words didn't make sense. "I left you a note. Didn't you find it?"

"I found it. 'Gone for a walk', doesn't tell me anything. Where are you? It's nearly nine o'clock. I've been worried about you for the past half an hour. How do you think I felt when I woke up this morning and found you gone?"

"But I left you a note."

"Do you think that makes it all right for you to wander around the streets?"

She wanted to say yes, but the tone of his voice made her think that wasn't the correct answer. "I've been bike riding every morning of the holidays. You know, exercising." She thought sticking with the excuse she'd given her mum might be the best plan.

"Exercising?"

She ignored the disbelief in his tone. "I didn't have my bike with me so I had to go for a walk instead."

"You-" He broke off abruptly before speaking again. "Hold on a minute. There's someone at the door."

She waited, trying to figure out what was being said. The words were distant, but not muffled so she guessed he held his phone at his side. It didn't help. She only caught three words. Appointment. Reschedule. Family. The door closed firmly.

"Are you there, Jena?"

"Yeah. Who was that?"

"Where are you? I'll come and pick you up."

"I'll be back soon. In about half an hour or so." She wanted to finish talking to Jack. Not that he was being helpful. So much for telling her he could help.

"Where are you?"

She knew that tone. The firm sound that let her know it would be pointless to argue. She nearly smiled at the familiarity. It had been a long time since she'd heard it. Eleven years. "Near my school. I can meet you out the front."

"I'll be there in ten minutes and then we can go shopping."

"But I haven't had breakfast yet."

"We'll get something while we're out. Ten minutes." Al hung up.

Jena stared at the phone for a moment before turning the light app back on. "I have to go."

"What are you going to do?"

She met Jack's gaze, trying not to worry about the concern she could see. "I don't know. I need to think about it." She'd barely got her dad back. She didn't want to lose him so soon. Actually, she didn't want to lose him ever.

"Don't take too long. An hour might be too late."

"We're going shopping. Everything should be okay. It's not like he's about to fall asleep while we're wandering about the shops."

"Don't count on it," Jack muttered. "I couldn't think of anything more boring than shopping."

A smile momentarily escaped. It vanished when she thought of her problems. She didn't know what to do. She almost hated Korbin's parents for taking him away when she needed him. "I have to go." She repeated her earlier words since she didn't know what else to say. "I'll-" She didn't want to see him later. From what he'd said she guessed he'd vanish when all her problems were over. "Bye, Jack." She slid between the wardrobe and the wall.

He followed her outside, stopping in front of the groundsman's shed after she'd closed the door. "I'll see you later."

There were those words she hadn't wanted to hear. "I hope not."

Jack chuckled. "I hope not too. For your sake."

With a nod, she strode to the front gate, sending a text to Korbin while she waited for Al. *I miss you. Your parents are cruel taking you away for so long.* She stared at the phone screen as it went dark, wishing Korbin could reply. He couldn't and didn't and she slid her phone into her pocket, wrapping her arms around herself as she waited for her dad. He was there in less than ten minutes, leaving the car running.

Al spoke before she'd closed the door. "Do you regularly take off like this? Don't you know how unsafe it is to wander the streets alone?"

She hadn't been alone. Not that telling him she'd

been talking to a ghost would have helped. She buckled up. "I'm starving."

"What time did you leave this morning?" Al pulled out onto the road.

She hadn't done anything wrong. "Mum doesn't go on like this when I go for a ride." She glared at her dad. "She encourages me to exercise. Says I spend too much time on the computer playing games with my friends."

"Do you?"

Jena looked out the window. She shouldn't have said anything. "Of course not." As if she'd say yes even if she did.

"Have you rung Patrice yet?"

"No."

"Are you sure?"

She looked towards him. Was that worry? Fear? She couldn't tell for certain. "Of course I'm sure. I was going to ring her after breakfast."

Al glanced towards her. "Didn't you tell her you were going to sleep in?"

Jena stared at him as she tried to think of what to say. The last thing she wanted to talk about was the reason why she hadn't been able to sleep. "I guess I'm already used to getting up early to start my day with some exercise." She really hoped that wouldn't turn out to be true. Sleeping in on weekends and holidays was one of her favourite things to do.

"Ring her now. Let her know you're okay."

"Why would she think I wasn't okay?" Had he rung Patrice when he'd found her note?

"Because she didn't want you to stay with me."

"Oh." She guessed that made sense, but she had the feeling there was more to his request than what he was saying. Mentally shrugging, she dialled her mum's number.

"What happened to sleeping in?"

Jena chuckled like she supposed Patrice expected. "What's with everyone wanting to know that answer? I think I'm in the habit of getting up early already. Maybe I shouldn't have decided exercising was a good idea."

Patrice laughed. "I'll be surprised if that lasts the entire holidays."

"So will I."

"Did you have a good night?"

The abrupt change in subject threw her for a moment. "Yeah."

"What happened?"

She heard the suspicion in her mum's voice. She'd waited too long to answer. "We went to the lookout and had dinner at the pizza place."

"That was it?"

She couldn't imagine telling Patrice that Al had held a knife at her throat. Especially with him sitting next to her. Maybe that was why he'd wanted her to ring now. "We had an early night."

"Now the early morning makes sense."

"Yeah."

"What are your plans for today?"

She wanted to demand why the interrogation. The thought of the knife kept her silent. "We're going shopping for things for my room."

"That should be fun." Patrice paused. "For you. Al always hated shopping."

"I remember." There were a lot of things she remembered. None of them involved knives. She had to stop thinking about it. But it was impossible with Al next to her and Patrice interrogating her.

"Call me tonight. Let me know how your day went."

"Okay." She didn't feel in the least bit like protesting. "Love you, Mum."

"Love you too."

# Chapter Fourteen



When Patrice hung up, Jena continued to hold onto her phone instead of returning it to her pocket. 'Tell someone, Jena.' Her grip tightened on her phone. Who? Her mum would stop her from seeing her dad. There had to be another option.

"Is everything okay?"

She glanced towards Al. "Yeah."

"Are you sure?"

What did he want her to say? That she hadn't been able to sleep since he'd held a knife at her throat? That as much as she loved him she was scared of what he might do? She was more scared of never seeing him again. She forced her lips into a smile. "I was trying to figure out what chance I would have of convincing you to let me have ice cream for breakfast. After all, I started my day off with a healthy walk."

Al chuckled. "It's winter, pumpkin."

"We don't have a real winter in Brisbane. Well, it doesn't snow."

"No ice cream."

"I wasn't planning on having it on its own. I wanted pancakes with it too."

Al chuckled again. "That doesn't sound much healthier. Okay. Pancakes it is. Light on the ice cream."

Jena smiled, catching his gaze when he glanced towards her. Now if only the rest of the day could go as smoothly as their conversation about what to have for breakfast.

When the laughter continued during breakfast, as they reminisced about the past, Jena began to think the day would only continue to get better. She was wrong. In the first shop they visited, Al complained that the sales assistant was stalking them. In the next shop he kept looking over his shoulder, making Jena feel nervous. No one had been behind them each time she'd checked. When she suggested going back to his place, leaving the rest of the shopping for another day, he'd said they'd continue.

A break for lunch hadn't been filled with laughter

like breakfast had been. Al had seemed jumpy, startled by every noise, glaring at the group of teenagers a couple of tables away. Recognising one of the girls, Jena had sat at an angle in her chair, hoping the girl didn't notice her.

When they'd finally bought all the items for her room, including a colourful mat that had needed a new bedspread to go with it, a flat pack desk and bookcase, as well as a couple of new books and ornaments for the metre tall bookcase, Jena had expected they'd go home. Instead, Al had checked the time on his phone and shook his head.

Jena checked her time. It was nearly four p.m. "What else have we got to do?"

"Groceries."

She eyed the back seat of the car. Not much else would fit in there and the boot didn't look any better. "Should we drop all this stuff home first?"

Al shook his head.

"Are you sure?"

"We're getting groceries."

She fell silent, turning her head to look out the window. She didn't want to go to another shop. If they stayed out much longer, she'd be the one jumping at shadows. Now if only they didn't need to buy much. "What do we need?" She looked towards her dad.

Al shrugged. "Bread, milk, the usual things."

"How can I help if I don't know what we need to get?" Or help speed things up.

Al parked the car at the grocery shop. "I'll worry about the basics and when we go down each of the aisles you can put in anything you think we might need."

That didn't sound like a quick shopping trip. She managed to hold back the groan that was her first reaction. "Okay." She got out of the car and waited for Al to lock it. The day was turning out to be much longer than she'd expected.

Inside the grocery shop, Al grabbed hold of a trolley and headed for the fruit and vegetable section. Jena trailed behind him. Several times she checked her phone as they went up and down every aisle, seeming to take an extremely long time to do so. And every time Al checked over his shoulder, she had to look behind as well. At least the grocery shop was crowded enough that there was always someone there.

The sound of tins smashing onto the floor had Jena turning to check what was happening. She didn't get a chance to see anything before Al was grabbing her and they were crouching on the other side of the trolley. "Dad?" Surely he wasn't going to lose it here.

Al stared through her for a few seconds before he blinked several times and stood up. He checked the time on his phone before returning it to his pocket and, grabbing hold of the trolley, headed for the front of the shop.

Jena stared after him for a moment. He didn't glance behind. She took a few steps towards him then broke into a run so she didn't get left behind. She joined him as he stopped in one of the lines, waiting to be served at a checkout. Several questions came to mind, but she pushed them away. This wasn't the place to ask those questions. Actually, she doubted she'd be able to ask them when they returned to Al's place. Checking the time she found it was a quarter to five. Far longer than it should have taken to put in the handful of groceries that were in the trolley.

By the time they were leaving the car park, it was five p.m. Going through the checkout had taken less time than it had taken for Al to put the groceries into the car. Jena didn't bother saying anything. She had no idea what to say. Actually, she had the strange urge to cry and wasn't sure why. Her dad was home and she was spending time with him. She should be celebrating.

Al pulled up in front of his house, holding out the keys. "You get the door while I start bringing things in."

Nodding, Jena headed for the front door, getting it unlocked before Al reached her side. "I'll get some of the groceries out of the car."

"How about you put them away while I bring them in."

Jena trailed behind him to the kitchen where he left the bags for her to sort out before returning outside. Seeing his wallet and phone on the table beside the grocery bags, she placed the keys with them. The corner of a business card stuck out of the wallet and she tried to tuck it back in so it didn't fall out. It was caught on something. Pulling it out, she noticed it was a card for a doctor. Was there something wrong? The sound of Al's footsteps had her sliding the card into a pocket of her jeans and putting the wallet beside the phone. There hadn't been time to put it away properly and she didn't want to be accused of snooping. Picking up one of the bags of groceries, she took it to the kitchen bench and began opening and closing cupboards as she tried to figure out where everything belonged. She didn't have half the things put away by the time Al finished emptying the car.

He stopped in the doorway. "I'll start assembling your furniture."

She glanced towards him, holding onto a cupboard door she held open. "Okay."

"Is everything all right?"

She had no idea. Why did he have the business card of a doctor in his wallet? "Yeah." Was he sick? Terminally ill?  She couldn't face him any longer. Not without fearing her thoughts would show on her face. Turning away, she peered in the cupboard, trying to decide if this was the correct one for the tin of soup sitting on the bench. Behind her she heard Al's retreating footsteps. When she heard him enter her bedroom, she straightened, looking towards the empty doorway. She needed to know what was wrong.

Hurriedly finding places for the rest of the groceries, she made her way to the bathroom, locking the door behind her. Sitting on the closed toilet lid, she pulled out the card and searched online for the doctor. Relief rushed through her when she discovered that Dr Eckert was a psychiatrist.  The relief was short lived when she found out she specialised in Post Traumatic Stress Disorder. Her worry returned and she tried to push it away. The only thing she knew about it was what she'd seen on movies and they had a tendency to exaggerate things. Surely it couldn't be that bad.

Guessing she'd been in the bathroom long enough, she returned her phone and the business card to her pockets and flushed the toilet to give her an excuse for having been locked in there. She slowly walked to her room, standing in the doorway to watch Al as he assembled the bookcase. Would the psychiatrist be able to help him? Would she be able to give her back her dad? She was about to return to the kitchen and put the card in Al's wallet when he looked up at her.

"You know you could help too. This is for you."

Hearing the humour in his voice, she forced a smile to her lips. "But you're doing such a good job of it that I didn't want to interrupt."

"Nice try. Get over here and help."

Jena joined him, trying to make sense of the diagram. By the time they'd assembled the bookcase and desk, they were smiling and it was dinnertime. Al suggested they call in for pizza. Jena wasn't about to argue. Not when things seemed to be going well again. And they continued to go well. She managed to return the card to Al's wallet without being caught, dinner was filled with laughter, they watched the television afterwards and Jena had an uneventful conversation with her mum before she went to bed.

That's when things stopped going well. She was woken from sleep by Al shouting. Reaching for her phone, Jena turned on the light app, shining it at the door she'd locked. What was she meant to do? After last time, she knew better than to wake him. But how could she leave him caught in his nightmare? It seemed wrong. Not knowing what else to do, she tried to go back to sleep, pulling the pillow over her head. It didn't help. She could hear the occasional shout.

# Chapter Fifteen

*Jena*

Stumbling out of bed, Jena decided to get a drink of water from the kitchen. Partway to the bedroom door, she turned back and pulled on her jacket, the cold floor reminding her she hadn't bought slippers. Using the light app on her phone, she opened the door and peered into the hallway. It was empty. Shining the light across the floor, she stopped when she reached the edge of Al's door. It was closed.

"No!"

She nearly dropped her phone. Fumbling with it, she accidentally turned the light off. Her heart raced at the sudden darkness and she tried to slow it down with deep, calming breaths. It didn't help. Standing in the darkness, she tried to make herself move. Instead she remained frozen, listening to the sounds coming from Al's room. They were interspersed by long moments of silence. Did she really need a drink?

Swallowing, her mouth dry, she decided she did. It took another couple of minutes before she could bring herself to walk to the kitchen, turning the light app on again. Her feet felt frozen and she was glad she was wearing her flannelette pyjamas Korbin had bought her as a joke. They were covered in tanks, a comment on what he thought of her gameplay. Playing as a tank was a perfectly acceptable game strategy as far as she was concerned, even if Korbin didn't agree. A thud from behind her had her spinning to face Al's door.

Everything remained quiet. The light timed out and she was plunged into darkness again. Taking a step backwards, she stared into the dark, unable to bring herself to look down at her phone long enough to turn the light on. She took another step backwards. Then another. When no more sounds came from the bedroom, she tried to force herself to look away. To turn on the light app so she could see where she was going. Another step had her running into the kitchen doorway. She moved to the side, about to turn away when the sound of the bedroom door opening had her freezing in place again.

"We have to get out of here." Al's voice was a harsh sound in the silent house.

Jena wanted to run back to her room and lock the door. Footsteps kept her from doing that. They came closer and closer. She looked around for somewhere to hide. The kitchen was full of shadows, a small amount of light filtering through from the window. The only place she could think of to hide was under the table and she'd have to move one of the chairs to do so. He'd hear her.

"What are you doing?"

For a second she thought he'd spoken to her. But he was in the hallway, passing the bathroom by the sounds of his footsteps. She had to go. Another glance around the darkened room had panic rushing through her. She had no idea where to go. The footsteps sounded closer. Holding her breath, she entered the lounge room, trying to step lightly. She was nearly at the front door when she heard Al crash into the table, swearing.

A glance over her shoulder was enough to show her he had the knife, the blade catching the limited amount of light in the kitchen. Jack's words came to mind and she almost felt the knife in her hand, the weight of it, the warmth of the handle after being held so long by her dad. 'I am dead because of her.

She stabbed me before I shot her. Deliberately stabbed me. Me shooting her was an accident. Do you want to be in that same situation?'

She had to get out of here. Holding her breath, she slipped her feet into her shoes, easing the front door open. Behind her she could hear Al trying to untangle himself from one of the chairs. She doubted it would take him long. As soon as the door was open far enough, she slipped outside and closed it behind her, leaving it unlocked. Locking it would have made too much noise. Not knowing where else to go, she walked towards the school, her heart racing and her arms wrapped around herself against the chill.

This was madness. She was wandering the streets of Brisbane, in the early hours of the morning, dressed in pyjamas. Tank covered pyjamas. How had everything gone so wrong? Her dad was alive, everything was meant to be perfect. Tears formed and she brushed them away when the cold stung her face. She wanted her dad. Not the man who'd returned. She wanted the man who'd told her to keep his jacket warm, who'd promised to return and had called her pumpkin as he smiled at her in a way that made her feel both loved and safe. She didn't feel safe.

Reaching the school she was relieved to find Jack waiting at the fence for her. "How did you know?"

She clambered over the fence, nearly falling on the ground.

Jack helped her straighten. "Ever since the angel said I needed to help you I've known where you are. Once I've helped you that ability will disappear along with your ability to see me." He guided her towards the groundsman's shed. "What happened?"

She really didn't want to talk about it. Didn't even want to think about it. But she guessed she needed to. Once she was seated in the space behind the wardrobe, on the cushion, she pulled up the details she'd searched earlier. The psychiatrist. Maybe this was the person she should be calling.

"Jena?" Jack sat down, waiting until she looked at him before he continued talking. "What happened?" He leaned back against the wall, drawing his leg up to rest his arm on it.

She sighed. "Everything is a disaster." She supposed it would be easier to tell Jack than some stranger on the other end of the phone. She held his gaze. "I thought I was going to die."

"Tell me what happened."

It took her less time to tell him than she'd expected. When she finished, she stared at her phone, fiddling with the edge of the case rather than face Jack.

"What are you going to do?"

She looked up at him, surprised to find he wasn't looking at her like she was an idiot. "Aren't you tempted to tell me, 'I told you so'? Not even a little bit? Or that I was stupid going back there."

# Chapter Sixteen



Jack smiled wryly. "You haven't done anything near as bad as what I've done. Not yet."

Jena didn't plan to. "I found a business card in his wallet." She told him about checking out the details of the doctor. "I think I should ring and talk to her." She hesitated. "I don't want to lose him. I want to be able to see him again. Just not the knife. Maybe she can figure it out. I mean, she specialises in PTSD. You'd think she'd know something."

"That sounds like a good idea."

Jena hesitated. But what if the psychiatrist agreed with her mum?

Jack frowned. "Except I'm still here."

"I was wondering if I should." It was her turn to

frown. "I forgot about that. I don't want to be stuck at school in the dark on my own."

"If I'm gone, you're safe."

"From everything or just my dad?"

Jack shrugged. "I don't know. That blasted bird doesn't tell me anything."

"Bird?"

Jack grinned. "The angel."

She couldn't resist returning his grin even though her stomach was in knots and she couldn't decide what to do. "I bet he loves that name," she said dryly

Jack chuckled. "Not as far as I can tell. So I'm going to keep on calling him that."

"To his face?"

"No, but I'm sure it doesn't matter. He probably knows anyway. He's an angel." Jack gestured to the phone. "What are you going to do?'

She stared at the screen, not sure. Before she could make up her mind, the phone started to ring. The display read 'Dad'. She hesitated, not sure if she wanted to answer. It continued to ring. She supposed she should get the call over and done with. "Hello, Dad."

"Where are you?"

She flinched at the anger in his voice. It wasn't her fault she'd had to leave the house. "You were-"

"Tell me where you are and I'll pick you up."

His words caused her to panic and she disconnected.

"Ring the psychiatrist," Jack said.

Not knowing what else to do, she did as he said, calling the number she found listed on the website. The phone rang several times before being picked up by an answering machine. The friendly female voice wasn't what she'd been expecting and she couldn't think what to say for a moment. "This is Jena Dutton, Albert's daughter. I found your card in my dad's wallet. I'm ringing you because-" She took an unsteady breath, trying to slow her racing heart. "Because I'm worried about my dad. Could you call me?" She rattled off her phone number and disconnected the call, turning the light app on. She stared at Jack. He was still there. "I thought you said you'd disappear once the problem was solved."

"Then it mustn't be. You're still in danger."

"But I rang the psychiatrist."

"I-" Jack's words were cut off by the ringing phone.

Jena stared at the display. Dad. She didn't want to talk to him. Didn't want him to pick her up. She couldn't get the image of the knife from her mind. She sent the call to her message bank, trying not to panic. What else could she do? Obviously nothing was working. Jack was still with her.

"Ring again. Tell the psychiatrist you need to talk. Mention the knife. Say you're hiding at your school. Say you're scared." Jack reached for her free hand when the phone started to ring again. "Don't tell your father where you are."

She again sent the call to her message bank, the phone falling silent mid ring. "Do you think I'm stupid?" Images raced through her mind. The knife featuring in all of them. "Actually, don't answer that."

Jack chuckled. "I don't think you're stupid." He sobered. "Now make the call and be convincing. You're not concerned. You're not worried. Are they the words you think of when you have a knife at your throat?"

"No." Terror was the closest she could come to describing how she'd felt. Terror and fear she'd die.

"Tell someone, Jena. Exactly what you feel."

Drawing in an unsteady breath, she rang the psychiatrist again. This time she was prepared for the friendly voice and spoke the moment it finished. "It's Jena again. I-" She took another deep breath before continuing. "I had to leave the house. He was wandering around with a knife. He had one last night. I thought he might kill me. He didn't know who I was. Then he did." She wiped at the tears that were running down her cheeks. "I don't want to lose him. I love him. I missed him when we thought he was dead." She gulped back a sob. "I don't want to die." The answering machine cut out and she lowered the phone, turning the light app on, about to speak to Jack.

He faded before her eyes, a smile forming as he disappeared.

"No." Jena shook her head. "I wasn't ready. You can't go. You can't-" The phone ringing interrupted her words. She stared at the screen. It wasn't her dad. Before she answered, she looked at the last spot where Jack had been. "I didn't get a chance to say goodbye." She lifted the phone to her ear. "Hello?"

"Is this Jena?"

"Yes." The voice sounded familiar. "Is this Dr Eckert?"

"It is. Are you safe now?"

The space behind the wardrobe was in darkness. No one knew she was here. At least no one living did. "I think so."

"Tell me what happened."

The words were so close to the ones Jack had said. 'Tell someone, Jena.' It made her feel like he hadn't left. Taking a deep breath, she did as Jack had said. She told someone.

## *Chapter Seventeen*

*Jack*

Jack was surprised to see Jena walking towards the groundsman's shed, holding a battery-powered lantern. It was the second last day of the school holidays and he hadn't expected to see her until Tuesday. It had been a week and a half since he'd last seen her.

She stopped in front of the shed and raised her hand as if to knock. She lowered it again, looking around.

When she remained there, not making a move to either get his attention or leave, Jack walked through the door, trying to make it swing open. Nothing happened. He tried again. This time it unlocked.

"Jack? Is that you? Are you here?" She opened the door and turned on the lantern before she entered. "This is a lot harder than I thought it would be." She closed the door before making her way to the space behind the wardrobe.

"If that blasted bird was a little nicer he'd let you say goodbye." If it was a punishment for him, he obviously wasn't the only one affected by it.

Jena raised her hand, with the lantern, slightly. "I brought this for you. It was lying around in the garage and no one has used it in ages. I thought you might find it useful. Well, not you, the people you are told to help." She paused a moment. "This is so awkward. I don't know if you're here. The door unlocking could have been you walking off because you didn't want to listen to what I had to say."

"I want to hear, Jena." He reached for the lantern, his hand going through it. Maybe he could interrupt it like he did the alarms on the classroom doors. He ran his hand through it several times, frustration and anger making his hand curl into a fist. The light flickered.

Jena stared at the lantern. "Was that you?"

"Yeah, but don't go asking me to do it again. It was hard enough the first time."

She turned the lantern in her hand, checking it over. "Maybe it's only faulty and that was wishful thinking." She shook the lantern. The light from it remained steady. "Can you do it again?"

Jack sighed. "You would have to ask that, wouldn't you?" Gathering together all of the anger he felt at the situation he forced his hand through the lantern. This time it not only flickered, but also rocked slightly. "I hope that's enough proof for you."

Jena grinned. "You are here. I wish I could talk to you properly. You know, seeing you and hearing you." She glanced at the lantern.

"Me too, Jena." He hated this. He liked that they came back. What he hated was not being able to talk to them and let them know how he felt.

"I wanted to thank you. For everything." She smiled wryly. "Well, except for that first night when you scared me." She fell silent again for a moment. "This is so much harder than I thought it would be."

"Just say the words, Jena. It's not like I can complain about what you're going to tell me."

"It's stupid really. Because you're probably the perfect listener now. No interrupting, no arguing, nothing." There was another moment of silence before she spoke. "I miss you, Jack. I know it was only a few days, but I do. I miss you. I feel like I've lost a friend." She slightly raised the lantern. "This is nothing compared to what you've done for me. For the advice you gave me. And I'm really taking it to heart. I feel like I've been telling everyone."

"I'm glad. About the advice, not about you missing me." If he was honest, he was a little glad about that too. After being forgotten for so many decades it was nice to be remembered.

"I'm going to a support group for the family members of those affected with PTSD. Dad goes to a support group too and is meant to see his psychiatrist a couple of times a week. He was meant to see her the afternoon we were out shopping. The support group is good. It's not so scary when I can talk to other people who've been through it. It's also good because it's only teenagers in my group. Well, there's one that's almost a teenager. They also aren't all military kids like I thought they'd be. Their parents all have different sorts of jobs. Police officers, paramedics, hospital staff, fire officers and some whose PTSD has nothing to do with their job. People who are victims of violent crimes and natural disasters. It's good to know I'm not alone."

"I know what it's like to be alone. I'm glad you're not."

"Korbin came back Friday and I told him all about it. I spent ages showing him different articles on the internet and he was annoyed with his parents and their timing for their holiday." Jena shifted from one foot to the other, momentarily looking at the floor.

"I didn't tell him about you though. I was going to. I know he'd believe me, but it seemed wrong to tell someone. Even my best friend."

"I have no idea how all this is supposed to work. If I'm meant to be kept a secret or if you can tell people. That blasted bird didn't tell me anything. I'm sure he's hoping I'll fail."

She glanced towards the wardrobe. "I should probably get going. I'm riding over to Korbin's house." She took a step back. "Oh, I nearly forgot. Mum isn't going to stop me from seeing Dad. She had a talk with the doctor and I'm not allowed to sleep over for now, but we're working on that. We're going to help Dad get through this. Help him become himself again. Not someone who's trapped by everything that happened to him."

"I hope that works out for you. For your dad and you."

Jena took out her phone and turned on the light app before placing the lantern on the floor and turning it off. "I'll leave this here for the next person who needs it."

She stayed quiet long enough that Jack thought she'd finished speaking. "Thanks, Jena. I'm sure someone will appreciate having a light in here."

"I can't help wondering that if you'd had someone

to tell everything to, things might have worked out different." She glanced towards the picture of Rose. "For both of you." She stepped backwards until she reached the wall. "Goodbye, Jack. I'm glad I had the chance to meet you."

He watched as she slipped between the wall and the wardrobe. "Goodbye, Jena." He didn't follow her outside. Instead he turned to look at the picture of Rose. He couldn't help thinking about Jena's words. If he'd had someone to help him through his grief, would things have turned out different? For both of them? He had no idea. "I'm sorry, Rose." The words felt as inadequate as always. He knew that nothing he said or did could ever make up for what he'd done. But that didn't stop him from trying.

# Free Ebook

Subscribe to Avril's newsletter to receive a free ebook. This ebook is exclusive to those on her mailing list. To find out more about this offer visit: http://www.avrilsabine.com/free-ebook/

*

We value your privacy and will not sell, rent, exchange or loan your email address to third parties. Your information is confidential and you are under no obligation to remain on the mailing list and can unsubscribe at any time.

# Acknowledgements

Thanks to the usual crew. For everything, including pointing out my mistakes. Without all of you my stories wouldn't be as good.

# To The Reader

If you enjoyed this book, why not consider leaving a review to help other readers discover it too? Reader engagement is one of the few ways that lets an author know readers want more books in a particular series or genre. So leave a review and tell friends, not only about this book but also about other ones you've enjoyed, so you can continue to enjoy books by your favourite authors for years to come.

Dreams are meant to be lived,

Avril.

# About The Author

Avril is an Australian author who lives with her family on acreage in South East Queensland. She writes mostly young adult speculative fiction, but has been known to dabble in other genres. You can find more information about her at her website www.avrilsabine.com where you can also subscribe to her newsletter to be kept informed about new releases, current projects, blog posts and exclusive news.

# Titles By Avril Sabine

Stories about strong characters and characters who discover their strengths.

**SERIES**

*Assassins Of The Dead- Young Adult Fantasy/ Paranormal*

Book 1: Dark Blade

Book 2: Dragon Touched

Book 3: Society Against Vampires

Book 4: King's Request

*Dragon Blood- Young Adult Urban Fantasy (with elements of romance)*

(5 book series)

Book 1: Pliethin

Book 2: Wyvern

Book 3: Surety

Book 4: Knight

Book 5: Mage

*Dragon Mage- Young Adult Urban Fantasy (with elements of romance)*

(Series two of Dragon Blood series)

Book 1: Promise

*Dragon Blood Chronicles- Young Adult Urban Fantasy (with elements of romance)*

(Companion stand alone series to Dragon Blood)

Book 1: Oath

Book 2: Betrayed

*Guardians Of The Round Table- Young Adult Fantasy LitRPG*

(Co-written with Storm and Rhys Petersen)

Book 1: Dexterity Fail

Book 2: Goblin Boots

Book 3: Singed Feathers

Book 4: Frog Mage

Book 5: Crystal Mine

Book 6: Cursed Harp

*Rosie's Rangers- Young Adult Western Steampunk*

(6 book series)

Book 1: Justice

Book 2: Vengeance

Book 3: Treachery

Book 4: Accused

Book 5: Wanted

Book 6: Corruption


*Mark Of Kings- Children's Fantasy*

(Upper middle grade/preteen)

(4 book series)

Book 1: The Arena

Book 2: The Island

Book 3: The Assassin

Book 4: The King

**STAND ALONE SERIES**

*Demon Hunters- Young Adult Urban Fantasy/ Horror (with elements of romance)*

Book 1: Blood Sacrifice

Book 2: Retribution

Book 3: Tainted

Book 4: Premonition

Book 5: Cursed

Book 6: Feud

Book 7: Extrication


*Plea Of The Damned- Young Adult Urban Fantasy/Paranormal*

(6 book series)

Book 1: Forgive Me Lucy

Book 2: Forgive Me Aiden

Book 3: Forgive Me Jena

Book 4: Forgive Me Kobe

Book 5: Forgive Me Marti

Book 6: Forgive Me Dawson


*Realms Of The Fae- Young Adult Urban Fantasy (with elements of romance)*

The Sword (short story in Like A Girl Anthology)

Heart Of Stone

Book 1: A Debt Owed

Book 2: Marked By The Hunt

Book 3: The Magic Collector

Book 4: An Unexpected Betrayal

Book 5: Imprisoned By Iron


*Fairytales Retold (Short Stories)*

Snow-White And Rose-Red

The Twelve Brothers

The Light Princess

Beauty And The Beast

Sleeping Beauty

Aschenputtel

The Golden Bird

The Frog Prince

The Death Of Koshchei The Deathless

*Myths And Legends Retold (Short Stories)*

Ion, Son Of Apollo

Sir Gawain And The Maid With The Narrow Sleeves

Princess Ilse, The Giant's Daughter

## YOUNG ADULT NOVELS

*Young Adult Fantasy (with elements of romance)*

Elf Sight

Earth Bound

*Young Adult Urban Fantasy*

Stone Warrior (with elements of romance)

The Jungle Inside

*Young Adult Contemporary (with elements of romance)*

Through Your Eyes

The Ugly Stepsister

Perfect Little Princess

*Young Adult Contemporary/Paranormal*

Whispers In The Dark (with elements of romance and same sex relationships)

Over Too Soon (with elements of romance)

*Young Adult Sci-Fi*

Experiment X-One-Six (Urban Sci-Fi/Superheroes)

An Endless Dawn (Post Apocalyptic Sci-Fi)

**CHILDREN'S BOOKS**

Dragon Lord (Preteen/early teens) (Fantasy)

The Irish Wizard (Upper middle grade) (Urban Fantasy)

**SHORT STORIES**

*Urban Fantasy*

Eternally Late

Dealings With Joe

Glimpses (short story in That Moment When
Anthology)

*Contemporary*

The Brat Next Door

*Fantasy LitRPG*

(Set in the same world as Guardians Of The Round
Table Series)

Tales Of Inadon 1: The Disc (Co-written with
Storm and Rhys Petersen) (short story in Game On!
Anthology)

*Post Apocalyptic Sci-Fi*

Compulsive Directive

**NONFICTION**

A Year Of Weekly Writing Exercises (Creative Writing)

Cooking For Families With Allergies (Cooking) (Co-written with Storm Petersen)

Tell Me A Story, Grandma (Memoir)

*For the most up to date details on available titles visit:*

www.avrilsabine.com/books/bibliography

# Plea Of The Damned Series

To learn more about this series visit:

www.avrilsabine.com/series/potd

**BOOKS AVAILABLE IN THE PLEA OF THE DAMNED SERIES:**

Book 1: Forgive Me Lucy

Book 2: Forgive Me Aiden

Book 3: Forgive Me Jena

Book 4: Forgive Me Kobe

Book 5: Forgive Me Marti

Book 6: Forgive Me Dawson

# Disclaimer

This is a work of fiction. Names, characters, businesses, places, events and incidents are either the products of the author's imagination or used in a fictitious manner. Any resemblance to actual persons, living or dead, or actual events is purely coincidental. The opinions expressed or beliefs held are those of the characters and should not be assumed to be the opinions or beliefs of the author.

www.ingramcontent.com/pod-product-compliance
Lightning Source LLC
Chambersburg PA
CBHW030835200726
48285CB00007B/2444